The Nihilist Overture

E. B. Roland

DISARTICULATED PRESS

Adelaide

First Disarticulated Press paperback edition September 2025

Disarticulated Press

disarticulatedpress.com

Roland, E. B.

Nihilist Overture

ISBN 9781764201971 (pbk.)

Foreword

It was always dank in the UniBar. Lowlights, rust red, beer-stained carpets, awkward plastic bar stools and a rickety old pool table. And everything had a ring stain from a dirty glass. All the smells of misspent youth gathered to create a permanent ripe musk: stale beer, acrid whiskey, sweat like off onions, vomit, premature ejaculate, weed and cigarettes. It was a place for the low lives, this dive on the top floor of the old campus building. Arguments, break-ups, one-night stands, hoots of laughter and clumsy high-fives. I remember it sentimentally, where the real lessons were learned, and quickly forgotten the next day.

The masturbatory pumping of the telescopic trombone tuning slides jerked and pulled, as the jazz band banged on, on a Thursday night. Packed to the rafters… Duke Ellington, Glen Miller and dollar beers. On the top floor, a sprawling balcony full of cigarette and weed smoke bellowed over the grassy lawns below, in front of the student union building. The nights would drag on, pouring our last

pennies into the bar till, feeding ourselves with warm ale
from a plastic cup, until the walls would bow, the floor would
lean out toward the high windows, dragging us in and out
from the bar to the rolled cigarette, the whiskey to the joint.
We would take refuge in the plastic booth with the steel
tables, painted black, watching the beer soak through the
carpets, up into an acrid foam, *up, up* until it was around our
waists and we were swimming, heavy legged, in the beer slop
run off of a sodden, drunk mind.

And maybe that's when I first saw him, swimming
through the slop, a determined hippopotamus with slicked
black hair, drug dealer shades and a novelty Hawaiian shirt.
Two beers in each hand above his head, he crossed the
Rubicon to our little booth in the rampant storm. He had an
odd band of groupies, old men in Akubras, a manic little
Asian man, a bevy of young girls. And his voice poured out
poetry, through each sip of his beer, a new truth to share in
his Chicagoan vernacular. Poetry, philosophy, politics, art,
famous novelists, music; it was all a haze of eagerly nodding
heads, gaping minds letting his words penetrate them, as the
conversation spewed out of the tops of our heads in plumes
of weed smoke over the balcony, late into the night. One
minute of conversation, and we were friends for life.

And so many nights after that, the same thing. The
drunkenness, the drugs, love, grief, beautiful women, respect.

Instant brothers in the wash of mediocre minds that just couldn't understand this kind of drunken nihilism. Because that's what it was; that is what he proselytised. I was all in. There was nothing else worth living for as much as that.

The hiss of the microphone through the headphones, the click, the pop. Countdown, and record… our wasted nights converted into poetry, music, spoken word. Some of these recordings still survive. There was *Things I Do That Other People Wouldn't*. It became scripture, a way to wade through the muck and come out unscathed. There were the drugs from the student dentist: some kind of bad tasting novocaine that did nothing at all, at least when you drank it. Shrooms in the city, talking toilet bowls, girls always hanging off him. Smashed pint glasses on the pavement, running from the bouncers. But I wasn't another groupie. He joined the band when we played at the dive bars across the city, sharing out portions of his spoken word to eager listeners all instructed to sit on the floor. And then, he was gone, back to America, his degree completed somehow, his past waiting for him to rejoin it. It was an ache, this strange hole in my heart, the empty stool at the bar. He was off getting married, living his best life, so I took his lead and made my way through mine.

I was in Paris, for work, when I reached out some years later. I was having a hard time, feeling lonely away from my wife. And the drinking hadn't stopped; I kept myself lubricated most days in a drunken haze. It was like nothing had changed when he got back to my message, just two wasters taking up space in the UniBar, solving the world's problems by not giving a shit about anything. But something *had* changed. He had stopped drinking, gotten himself fit and was working his way through a world of sobriety trying to find a foothold for a better life with his new wife. It is this era that was his most prolific. The old, drunken recordings have mostly disappeared, maybe we forgot to press record and they never existed. Shards of poetry remain that he kept locked away in his laptop, his nihilist overture hidden away from the world. Over the next ten years, he added to it with poetry, songs, limericks. He created an entire oeuvre of work that had its beginnings in his juvenilia but was really formed in his dedication to sobriety and clarity of thought. Ten years later, we talk most days from across the globe. We've worked on projects together, music, sound and poetry. We both kept writing, even through years of disconnection. So, it is with great happiness and pride that I am able to help publish his work now, after all these years. His poetry has changed, his work more precise and immediate, but his philosophy has not. That was always there, lurking in the UniBar, speaking smoothly through shots of whiskey and puffs on his joint. Yes, he taught me the way of drunken nihilism in our younger days. Now I am learning the music and poetry of it, a nihilism born of experience, wisdom and recovery.

\-   Greig Thomson

\-   4th of September, 2025

(2004 - 2015)

In this time of my life I was mostly intoxicated, disillusioned, seeking, craving, consuming, and burning. It is marked by death, travel, drugs, drink, and confusion, but also love, moments of joy, truth, and friendship. The choosing and editing stage was difficult in that I now find much of this material awkward and unreflective of my current mind. That said, I tried to include as much as I could to give an honest reflection of where I was mentally and emotionally regardless of how embarrassing I might find it. Of course I didn't add the total garbage, ragingly offensive, and items with subjects that might recognise themselves.

There is a disorganized charm to this collection, though. My files were unorganized and scattered. As a result, the order is curated instead of chronological. At the time I wasn't living chronologically.

Enjoy,

Ed

Finally

There are no walls but those you build

The ground is always cold

Lay your head and breathe it in

You are finally alone

Life Stares Back

Wake up in bed

Text message

Cell phone chirping

Read a book of poems until they don't make sense

Turn on the kettle

Roll a cigarette to disguise the taste

Of stale cigarettes

I never feel good in the morning

The smoke escapes me

As I sit here typing

What will today bring?

And what will I bring?

The pains from this week have

Got me

Feeling old

Shoulder sore from a fall off a roof

Knee bashed from a crash

I don't remember

Head sore

From lack of memory

Can't get fucked anymore

Teases and tries

These are all of my mornings

These are the days that

Life stares back

Pretend

Expanding seas

Pretend to miss me

I can only miss violently

Moment to moment

Like the hunger inside

I will soon fulfill

My plastic fantasy

It's so hard

Not to believe

In poetry

Far Away

I pick up a book

Hope and want

Forgotten

Left for another day

Far, far, far away

4000 cocktails on a warm summer day

0 left undrunk

I miss home

There's hope for you

I worry about losing

Or my mojo running out

Drunk again

And on my way

To the greener pastures of
Far, far, far away

Please Skip This One

And now I sit on a plane

I am drunk

And feeling like a madman

I have no money

But I spend like a saint

I can only babble

I can't write

I am angered

By the thought that someone may read this

And I hope that they do

And the pain left on the page

Of a failure at what he loves

We only live one life

And this is the one I have chosen

I hope no one watches

As I tap and tap

The life I left behind is

Right in front of me

The Giant

There was a woman there that made me think

She was carrying a sleeping child

I wondered

How good would it be

To have a giant carry you while you slept?

I saw that

Child

Not weeping or laughing or weeping or dying

Well it was dying

But

I saw it

On its back

In its mother's arms

Sleeping

And I felt

Okay, OK

We chatted and we were drunk

I worried about judgment

I always do

I worried about what his people would think

When I got here with nothing

Slept in a park

Ate their food

And soaked up their wine

I wondered what they think

About this man

They had only known

This leech

I am not a bad man

And I know it

But…

I am a wreck

A shell

A farce

Do I deserve to be here?

I am here

Drunk again

At some friend's home

Typing away

Working on notes

More poems

My life away

Writing

Why?

Okay

OK

I have been rambling

I have been faking

I wonder if tomorrow

I will feel good

And where will it take me?

No point

No real thought yet

I will try to write

I will try to get a story out

I will try to be a writer

But I only tap

Tap

And where will that take me?

They don't know me

No one does anymore

Not I

Am I even real?

I often wonder if I am just making it up

From a hospital bed

Somewhere

My mother sitting over me

My family

Hoping I work it out

Hoping I come to

But I also

Think

That if this is the case

I have done well

I have made the friends

I have created them

Not so bad I guess

It's Just

It's all just writing

Regardless of the quality

Content

Place

Time

Love

I can't wait

To see what I create or destroy

Maybe I can be a virgin

Maybe I can be a nun

Maybe I can fall off a bridge

And wake up the next day wondering

If it really happened

Have I lost touch?

Am I insane?

And tomorrow comes

After I sleep

Good Day

I found today

Placed before me like a game

I could

Not

Really

Play

I cleaned a salt water pool

I sat in the heat

I walked the dogs

I talked to a friend

I had a good day despite my nerves

In a park

On the street

Drain

They eat a chunk from me every time I look

Every time I sip at a wine

Every time I give a hug,

Or get a phone call from someone who lost a loved one

Due to choice or inevitability

I hope I can keep on

I hope it all comes to a head

Before it breaks

More Arms, More Teeth

And I was right

I kept it going

Kept it rolling

Scamming

And floating

I ravaged the kindness of others

Drinks flowed

Drugs flowed

And gave

The mind

Peace

And the rest

It's all left to be betrayed

Forgotten

I wish I had more arms

More teeth

More everything

And this poem can go on forever

And it never has to end

This poem is a novel

I don't even know

What I write about anymore

I have

Sat

For years wondering

Searching trying

But as it goes

I've done

Alright

I always

Feel

The weight of everything

On me

I try hard

You know

But it gets too much

Couplets Hand in Hand

All the smiles

Aimed anywhere

And the lies

That we tell each other

We are all

Only one

The moment

The pain stops

Staring and wondering

How we spend our time

Short walks

And the longer ones

How many paths we exclude

For every step we take

And the nerves

And the anxiety

For the change

We all go through

Never know

When to forget

When to hate

To hope

Who is it now?

They float through

Door knocking

Chattering

Child's heart

Smiles

Horror and death

Crying and crying

Lost visions

Forgotten friends

Memories

Like traffic

I Am Not

And I hoped

For more but

I just sat as usual

Writing

Until I couldn't think

I looked for inspiration

I looked for love and harmony

I looked and I looked and I

Looked

But there was nothing there but

Insecurities

I can't worry for you

I can only worry for myself

Which is more "I have no idea"

And people hate poetry

They think it reeks of babble

It is

About honesty

But there is no more to it than that

What I have is immortal

What I have is life

I may be an artist in the way I live

I may be an artist in the way

But I am not an artist

I am not an artist

I am not an artist

Bucket List is a movie from the 90s.

Ain't got no bucket list

No dream job

No dream home

I don't dream like that

Feels like chores, holding up these

Heavy

Heavy dreams

Working on that list

"Gotta go to Fiji or die unhappy..."

*Could've been coming home exhausted from my dream job
to my dream house with my dream partner, only to die
without going to Fiji.*

Fuck Fiji, man

Fuck that job

Fuck that house

Your dreams and lists will

Get in the way

Of a good life

Bob

There was once a flower that was the only flower of its kind in a great field.

The plants and other flowers that surrounded it accepted it as it was.

They thought the little flower was beautiful.

They didn't want to bother it

It was many colours long

It felt satisfied with its beauty

The problem was it was stuck to the ground

It couldn't seek out other flowers of its kind

It could not seek other flowers that were long like the sun is hot and colourful like the water is powerful

So, it sat there

It sat there unwilling to accept its fate

The flower gave itself a name

Bob

"My name is Bob"

The flower thought to itself

So Bob waved in the wind and sought no attention

But attention was bestowed regardless of Bob's intentions

Bob knew that he was the prettiest flower in the whole world

Bob had babies

His pistil and stamen communicated without emotion and
seeds did flourish

In the late spring Bob spread his seeds and they all found
purchase in the fields around

Bob's offspring were all just as pretty as Bob, but they made
themselves no names, for they were, at that time, but one in
many

They had no need for names

They all were happy being one of the prettiest flowers in the
field

Bob hated this

He wished they all knew their importance as one of the
prettiest flowers in the whole world

He decided that these offspring were not enough and he
worked and worked, though and thought, and realized that
he must grow legs

He must grow legs, travel to a warmer climate, and make more pretty, pretty flowers that should be renowned, revered, adored

And do this Bob did

He traveled the world and made millions of the most pretty fucking flowers the world had ever seen

They were picked, displayed, and revered as they deserved

But still, Bob was the only flower with his own name

This made Bob very sad

Eventually there was a great war of balls of fire, and all the flowers were gone

Bob lived to watch all but the ugliest flowers die

And then eventually even the ugly ones died

Bob blamed himself for the war

He could have stopped it

He could have done something

But he just withered and died

His colors faded first

Then his stem lost pressure and he bent at an awkward angle

His unlikely mind withered

He became quite an ugly sight

His last thought was a guilty one

Do you feel bad for Bob?

You shouldn't

He is everyone you pretend to hate

A Very Short Biography

I lived a part of my life

Crying at the circus

Grasping at my mother's hand

Being blown about in time

I lived a part of my life

With my face washed in the snow

A bully's angry bleeding hands

Helping me along

I lived a part of my life

Freezing in a small room

With a million darling cubicles

Containing rage and boredom

And I remember when it meant something

I remember when I tried

But for lying and the crying

And a bag around my shoulders

A head full of confusion

And a mind full of joy

What happened to me then

I can only remember now

I lived a part of my life

Drunk on stolen whiskey

Walking hand in hand

My heart made of granite

I lived a part of my life

Shifting in a fistfight

Tripping in a graveyard

And learning Mexican

And I remember trying to forget

About all the small regrets

But hearing Willie Nelson sing

Or the soft creases in a woman's face

I hoped freedom would find me

Down the road somewhere

But what happened to me then

I can only remember now

And I lived a part of my life

Suffering up and down the hills

Working for a pig

Saving money for possessions

I lived a part of my life

Getting stoned in a car

Driving towards the sunrise

Eyes bleeding from the pills

I lived a part of my life

Dressed in gowns and twitching

Screaming for the women

Who left me half a man

And I can only remember

The things that happened then

A force so strong, it took ten years

To see it back again

And I was falling in a river

The night's warmth on my back

… A woman I loved

And some cheap red wine

I lived a part of my life

Standing in the sun

And sitting by a tree

Sometimes I knew the world was spinning directly with my whim

And years have passed

Face full still of snow

In such a lovely place

I wished I was a farmer

Or anything I'm not

I wished I had learned Mexican

I wished that the first time I smelled love

It hadn't been so frightening

I lived a part of my life

Strong and unafraid

When the balance hit me right

And true joy was within me

Presence

Hands up

Feet down

Head high

Life swollen

Legs sore

Head swollen

Heart heavy

Breeze drifting

Hands up

feet down

Head high

Breeze drifting

Head soar

Feet tripping

Sans meaning

With purpose

Hands tripping

Head sore

Breeze dribbling

Heart expanding

Hands down

Breeze explaining

Feet down

Its raining

I'm seeing

And waxing

It's lost

It's found

Head high

Mind drifting

Head soaked

Feet hard

Mind drifting

Time passing

Caught fetching

Feet drifting

Mind passing

It's pouring

Time gone

Brain swollen

It's time

It's over

But wanting

And breathing

With purpose

And knowing

Feel wet

And heading

Towards life

Exploding

Dancing is for Idiots

Dancing is for idiots

People with guts.

Night coloured sculptures in the dark sweating

What happened to us

I stared at her

It'll be fine

You don't understand me

You don't want me to

Am I a child?

Stop picking at it

At what?

You know

Singing is for thinkers and idiots

Dancing for those who know better

... *Doing Almost Anything*

I could be

Trying to get laid

Eating peanut butter

In total silence

There are many things

I could be doing

but I choose to do this

I could be

Trying for truth

Choosing a religion

Chaotic noises of the street

I choose to do this

At a graveyard

In a bingo joint

In mother's kitchen

In law school

At court

At work

At the end

In love

In denial

I choose to do this

I am doing this

But daydreaming

Of another life

Youth

And it comes to where

The cattle die

The childhood freezes your mind

It was all wonderful

Glorious with the woman you love

And when Mom used to talk to you

From her heart

Dad had the wind

To play ball

The money was good for the job

You didn't have to worry

Hope

Watching a film about a tortured artist

Wishing and hoping

My dreams of poetry

Write

Paint

Creation

The man in me left

With the hopes

The man in me stays for the

Flesh

And the hope is for?

And the hope it breathes

What are we meant for?

And what are we?

So I can be hoping

Looking into the dreams of a genius

Thinking too hard

About what it is to be one

How it Feels

In these days of struggle

As all days are

You have to ask yourself

You have to know

How does it feel?

Feels good, baby

It feels like a million butterflies

Perched, flapping on my scrotum

I couldn't be gladder

That people are dying

Couldn't feel more safe

Knowing

That there is so much violence

Far, far, far away from me

I just met a girl

On dollar beer night

Who's struggling?

How Much We Can Take

In this lovely and lonely world

We all have

Responsibilities

But to whom?

Listen to the lies of your parents

Listen to the lies of your government

Listen to the lies of your church

And your school

And your friends

And how much can we take?

When can we stop listening?

When you wake up early and smell the cool fresh air

Slowly becoming

Poison gas of industry

And the lies in your heart stifle your breath

Your heart

Your mind

Your imagination

We have but one chance

Sever the tie

Turn off the television

Ignore the problems

The wars

The chanting

The right and the wrong

Accept it

It's not going anywhere anyway

The problem with politics and systems of that

Nature

*Is that

Without

Problems

*There

Is

No

*Need

*For

*The

System

So, They must assure problems

Fear

Hatred

War

There is no money in unity and love

There is no money in peace

There is no financial future in the future

So, take a breath

Exhale

And focus within for freedom

It can't exist outside

Your heart

Out there all is burned and forsaken

In here is warm and free

Join us

The revolution has begun

And you don't even have to fight

In this revolution

Just give your love to those you already love

And it begins

He and I

I didn't know him

He wouldn't let me in

He cheated he lied

But I thought he thought

He did not

And I was sinking

He was a writer I think

But he never did write

And we talked about fractions

And books without endings

There was a glow to him

He didn't think poets knew

Anything, nor did the prose

Work for us now

Or before to help him

I loved him and do

He thought I was stupid

I may have known more

But he never looked

Then there was the drink

It ended everything

We never did stop

It's still right here with us

The jerk in the store

And the girl with the cleavage

People look happy

But he thought they all lied

But there's still tomorrow

He will still be there

With me

Watching

If I loved myself

I would have killed him

When I had the chance

And the courage

New Us

I'm gonna do it, baby

I am

First thing tomorrow

I'm gonna wake up

Brush my teeth

Shave

Eat a good breakfast

With strong coffee

I'm not even gonna smoke

Pot tomorrow

Remember

I don't care if I talk now

I don't care if I walk

If I breath

Or stink

Or feel

Or listen

Because tomorrow

It's all gonna change

The rivers will run with shimmering gold

The wind will feed my soul

My belly will be full with

Expensive foods and spices

Tomorrow I take charge

Tomorrow, baby

I'll make you happy

I'll smile from noon to night

I'll just finish today with a quick drink

Just a bottle of wine

To celebrate

The new us

I love you

I Just Want to Do Something…

Should I write the way I feel?

Act? Should I act?

Maybe I can get enough followers

But how do I get those?

I am so discouraged

But happy under it all

I feel so lost

And I can't help but blame

My mind's evolution

Not keeping up

With the world around

Familiarity skewed by the faces

Brought to you by

Brought to me by

You?

Them?

It is all so confusing

That I could see a thousand strangers

And not recognize my neighbour in the bunch

Doesn't this have an effect?

It seems it would

It seems that I would have

But no one is watching the hill

And the clutter rolls down

I just wanted to do something

I just don't know what it is

Inside me feels like

An army of mountains

Moving at the speed of sound

Like it is on

Some alien terrain

While I just watch on

Confused

Grave

Mark my grave

Give my life a name

Don't call me nothing

For I was a force

Bury me deep

Deep in the clay

And when my flesh

Is eaten away

Let my bones rest

Rest where they lay

In my neatly identified grave

My name proudly stated

Maybe a little vase

At first filled with flowers

But as the years pass

The flowers stop coming

The final ones rotten

In an inch of water

The stone even dulls

And over the years

My name and my dates

Can no longer be read

The bones now brittle

And what did I mean

But to the people I knew

For my short time here

A blank slate of granite

Once as proof and carved

As the man who lies under it

Like the rain from a cloud

Jelly

You can't help but do it

You have no options

Time passes

You should be happy you've had as long as you have

You managed to make it all

The way through adolescence

And you will keep tramping

There are only so many paths

They are a sticky jelly

Attached to your skin

Burning and hoping

It adds up to

Death in the end

And goodness and evil

That's where it all ends

Enjoy the scent of flowers

Through the doorway

From the can

It all seems so useless

All the screaming on campus

Talk of change

Dreams compromised

Only one to attain

While this is

While it happens

You can't ever see the joy

The truth

Life is

And it will

And it can

Remember that goals are

Versions of

Dreams

But the dreams

Were much better

And tomorrow

You can write to yourself

Again

Dusty

You're away

I've been alone a while

I have so many pictures of you

Stuffed away in my files

Some we took together, smiling

Some you never knew I took

Some of them got printed up

And placed into a dusty book

We have been so many places

Our lives lived side by side

These pictures prove it

You are away

But in my heart, and my mind

You reside

I am never alone again

Because I love you now

I love you still

The Greatest

I am the world's greatest writer

Be it a poem

A short story

A song

A letter to my niece

Can't help but be

Greatness

I am the world's greatest writer

Therefore, I have not the burden

Of idolization

I idolize no artist

No man

No one

I envy not

I want not of other lives

When my ink applies itself

To paper

Exactly the words

And only the words

That I want

Are etched

I am the world's greatest writer

For how could I not be?

I am the only writer that I want to read

You can be the world's greatest writer

Do you know how?

You

This is for you

I don't know who you are

I don't know your family

I don't know your country

I don't even know if you are living, dead

Or unborn

This is to you

This world is not made for you

You will suffer through it

The others will make you disintegrate

But I want you to know this

I have faith in you

I believe you can do what it is you are trying to do

Be it riches, fame, poverty

Or a fast and fun death

I know you can do it

I know that there is a place there for you

Despite all the things that your mind

And your parents

And your teachers

And your bosses

And coworkers

And strangers on the street

And bartenders

Tell you

You can submit

You can fight

But if you don't want to fight

You *will* fail

You *will* wake up one morning and find yourself

Truly naked

The job you have will define you

(What do you do?)

(I am a phrenologist)

I don't care if you want this advice

I don't even know if it is advice

But at least I took the time to give it to you

My only true friend

The Only Dance I Know

I know what it's not but I do it

For I could not learn another

I pretend it's tragic

It is the only dance I know

Sometimes I feel good

And I try to change it

A move, a jab step, a subtle twist

But it's still the same dance

I know

I try

And don't

But I like it for now

I am comfortable

I don't want to change it

When I feel old

When I feel poor

When I feel done

When I feel

I may change

The Destination

The destination is death

The ride is life

So what means more?

The end or the beginning?

A short trip is better if it takes longer

I remember the trips that took forever

A four-hour journey across town

A four hundred-mile trip in a saddle

A ten thousand-mile trip to nowhere

A week walking

Blisters on my feet

Doubt in my heart

Worry under my every thought

Or a four-hour flight to where I thought it was I wanted to be?

Most people want to get there

I want to do the getting

The beginning is important

The middle is the most important

Because that is where we are

We're in the middle

Stuck between the start and the finish

We are now

How do you like the end of this poem?

Is it the poem that you wanted?

Standing Up

Speeding through life with tin speakers in our ears

Hair falling in our eyes

The smell of malevolence

Attacking our noses through

Television screens

Childish dreams fall like leaves

Hints at misconduct that

Arouse us

In the heart of an artist

The blind eyes of a seeing man

The whim of a bird

The dance of its feather with the wind

An answer can be found

There is no life

In that which leads us to a predictable tomorrow

Comfort is death

All encompassing

Frightening

Treacherous

Careful

A goal is a fart in the cosmos

If you can't fuck standing up

Do it lying down

If not lying down

Don't fuck

Language

It's a funny thing with our language

How the low tend to get high

That in order to find one you must find the other

But to ourselves we must lie

Cuz we started high and found low again

Or we started low and found high

So you get to pick one

Where are you now

If it ended tomorrow

Where would you die?

Radio

Radio playing

A woman breathing

The ones that left

All sitting

Watching

While I try

Feel the nothingness

Look around

Are you like them?

Who are they?

Alone is not real

Try to write

You'll see how

It all falls in the end

Suicide Machine

Some new people gonna like old movies and

Some old people gonna like new shows but

It ain't easy to know what someone's like

To look at the style of their clothes

It's best to assume

They're as smart as you

As hard as you

Been through too much

It's best to guess

At sadness behind all eyes

Tough days and cloudy skies

Are coming for us

You can't blame them

They thought they were teaching

They believed what they learned

And they had no idea

That it was a suicide machine

Made just to trample and trounce

Their parents built them one

Their parents before them

They celebrated with ice cream

You succeeded in the suicide machine

You learned to hold in every scream

Hold in those unrealistic dreams

We pose

We preen

To please the suicide machine

What we left behind

It was our unrefined

Unglorified sense of self

No

I'm not broken yet

Not stuck too deep

This suicide machine

Is holding my hand so tight

Nature

The air in the sky

The water in the stream

The fire in the woods

It's destroying everything

But just like us

It's only rebranding

It's like the side of a bus

With law advertising

And in the future we'll see

The mountains breaking

The seas turn to ash

Halting the swimming

And just like you

It's ambiguous

Your kindness eschews

The lawyer on the bus

Our infinite space

And my imagination

They're intrinsically linked

This has only begun

Believe me,

Believe me,

Believe me,

Believe me,

It's not just a fantasy

For us it's so real

And when you forsake me

I know it won't break me

But I know it will take me

Some years to recover

I love you

Mastery

Shattered brain convulsions from lust unreconciled

With a handful of self-pulsing and chumping

Till death do us part

I wish for more

And find ever less

Self-sacrifice to the gods of disillusionment

Pearly ropes

Like a god's white fangs

And now I need no more

Just a drink

(2016-2025)

I quit drinking in 2013. I quit smoking weed in 2016. My
organization improved. My focus improved. My life
improved. The poems from these stages are organized
chronologically.

Alcohol cessation made it very hard to write for several years.
My mind was lost. I couldn't get anything down, and when I
did it had no life or chaos. Eventually thoughts swarmed
back, but it took time and consistency.

I had to sit down to write, often with no ideas, and often to
find the writing of a quality and style that I didn't appreciate.
Looking back now, I wish I hadn't trashed all of those pieces.
I think it is likely that some had worth that my mind could
not accept. Even if they were as bad as I imagined, it would
have made contrast.

There are many cliches that fit what happened to me. Things
have to break to be repaired, before you get organized you
must disorganize. You can choose your favourite.

I know now that defining myself through anything outside of
the mirror and my thoughts, especially drugs and materials, is
a road to a questionable destination, with wonderment to see
on the way.

The Words that Follow

The menacing words

Touching my heels

Follow me still

My sword it is steel

As is my resolution

My God he is real

He teaches me to deal

with the words that follow me

To my extinction

You can't fight words with words

You need to have violence

They stack up behind you

Vicious malevolence

I tried to impart

Some rules from my heart

To the heart of these words

And their meanings

But despite all my efforts

They fuck with me - follow me

I swear I will cut these words

Into letters

I will chop out their insides

Gut them exactly

Like a seer with ten eyes

Still seeing blurrily

It is not harmless

It is not jumping rope

A hula hoop airbag

A pro without hope

Jump at me, mean words

Just once you can see

That I am unflappable

No word means 'me'

Not even I

I know Dawn

She sleeps on my chest

She sucks out my breath

She feeds me incest

She fucks, I repress

She slips off her dress

I digress

She holds me in fear

Wrecks me with love

How she drinks so much beer

Sour breath like a dove

It's weird

Her love

Like pity

Or hate

But I can't complain

Because she's there every morn

With a box full of porn

Lost and forlorn

To feed me her scorn

With pussy

And violence

Madness

And hate

A forgotten love state of the dead

I just hope that the fuck of the world

Has my back

Because I

I do this the way

The fuck of the world

Asked me to

So when the time comes

To punch my last timecard

To have my last smoke

To savor my last moments

The fuck of the world

Better soothe me

It better move me

It better promote my movie

Cuz I did it the right way

Like a great giant

Like a pillar

A beacon

A ray of darkness illuminating

The fuck of the world

Better have my back

In the end

Today the world is mine

I eat my fill

Shit it out

And now I rest

Shrunk

You may think you know

From what I say

But where it goes

What it knows

It's a result of where I been

States

Of being

I'm being

Held

Not

Lover held

Kept warm

Safe, in fiery arms

I'm being held

Against

My will

Not a living will

That splutters in the night

Waking at dawn

Committed

If you can't get this

If you think me unsafe

Then you don't know what safety is

You don't understand

Despite your smartish brain

And your training

And all those moneys

In the brittle banks

Fragile with glass walls

It's me that fights this fight

It's me you want to be

Here me blow

As I take a bow

And exit stage left

Heau Beaus

You have a smoke halo

Only the hobos can see

And what a fine fellow

With a glass of whiskey

Keep your chin up, though

Even though that's a good way

To get it punched

Another week to get high cuz your low

You gotta guitar there?

You gotta notepad?

You gotta keep your wits about you

Hobos and time travellers

Looking for your mind

Because it's not just unquiet

It's uncommon

Starving Clouds

Can it feed the abandoned hope?

Can it lengthen the rope?

Might it get me off dope?

Give beauty to my lope?

Will it make her love me?

Will it make him respect me?

Can it make me trustworthy?

Let me fall asleep at ten-thirty?

Will I know what's behind the stars?

Will I find my way home from the bars?

After I left her there in the car?

Crying about where we are?

What can money do to help me now?

Now that I'm alone?

Now that the light that once shone

Is now dark?

I am swimming in the ocean

It's turning to lava

The clouds have visible ribs

They're starving and dying

They're turning to smoke

I'm seeking my own mind

Fingers wringing in stress

Ears ringing, you're singing

Still we distract

The point is out there

Floating in the distance

I can only swim so far

And in swimming you must

Only go half as far

So you can return safely

But how am I supposed to know?

In still lava

Clouds are smoke

They're hungry

Starving

You can see their ribs

Am I a man lost at sea?

Or am I an island?

I'm unreachable

By any vessel

But heart

And soul

Lava can't melt that

We'll be fine

You and I

As long as we keep our rhythm

Keep our time

It is all we have

And as it passes

I wonder where halfway is

Or where it was

Cow

Fuck the What

The why

The how

I got half a mind

To fuck a cow

If I Could

If I could wade in the lava

Float in the sand

Hear the trees sing

Feel the cut of sharp breezes

If I could

Walk on the ocean

To get to the land

Feel warmth

When I hold your hand

If I could I would

Fall asleep at the wheel

Dream a dream unreal

And fall out of sleep

To the crash of crashes

And see you there

Dressed in red

Titties blazing

Teeth shining in smiles

Legs like pow

I could then

I could do anything

I could live in my death

I could live with yours

But for now

I'll dream of a lava bath

And wait

Gotta get out of here

Whole and quick

So much work to do

Too much shit to fix

The wind it howls at Me

Like she's in pain

Slaps at me

With her cold harsh rain

I feel to much

Too charged up

Like a battery of pain

Leaking a wordless refrain

A howl from the sky

A scowl from this guy

Three Dirty Limericks

There was an old dog from LA

Whose dick learned to speak, sing, and play

But when it got literate

It wrote "Fuck dirty limericks!"

"I'll take a haiku any day!"

There was once a man from Wisconsin

Who's name has long been forgotten

But his dick, it lives on

In the annals of song

Up there none forget a great johnson

A living man crafted a poem

To convince a young lady to blow him

But when she did sneeze

He dropped to his knees

For she blew his cock through his colon

"Boom," Said He

He always said "boom"

To the girls in the room

It was just his thing

And that flat diamond ring

It was gaudy and blue

And the rain it flew

Through the window until

We shut it but still

It felt breezy in there

And the girls would swear

That their tits could cut glass

But he'd spank their ass

And scream "no way"

"Can't gonna snow today"

"It can't gonna rain more"

Said his girl Lenore

She was named for the poem

But he just said "boom."

Xenonic Death

Fuck all these crumbs

That fall on my chest

Like little toy soldiers

That bleed through their vests

Like marks in the sky

What is even real?

The ground smells like dog farts

And rotting orange peels

My ribs are jutting

Out from my neck

They choke me and freeze

All the sick and infected

Diseased and distracted

Farmers they're dying

They're crying

Like pale folks locked in a cage on the sun

With nothing but rum

To drink under the frozen

Sky

The fire inside

Stays doused

Who are these guys?

What the fuck do they want?

With their damned empty eyes

And the flies buzz about

The soldiers in the sun

The pales and the guys

They run and have fun

With the leftover girls

They're lost in this world

Forgotten for years

But at least we had beers

You fool of a man

What was the plan you had?

Did you know that the hands

Of God were so bland

As to give you this life?

This curse in the sun?

This bleeding fat chump

With his pimples and rump

Fat with the bumps

On his dumb fucking head

He's already, dead

In the end we all go

But some never existed

And my time may be here

Cruel, happy, untwisted

I'm living this out

To choke down my last breath

I want a last minute

I want a last second

I want half of that, too

It's Not That Cold

"It's dark

"No, it's fine. I can see

"You can see, but it's still dark

"The moon is here

"It's cold

"It's not too cold

"I can't feel my fingers

"Yes you can

"Fine

I can see them and feel them

That's not the point

"What is the point?

"I'm unhappy

"But we're here

Together

And it's light enough

It's warm enough

"Enough for what?

"Enough to be happy

"But I'm not

"Why?

"Because

"Why, though

"Because it's dark and cold

"But...

"I know

Enough

That's what I've had

I've had enough

"So what?

You *wish* it dark?

You *wish* it cold?

"I wish it was nothing

I wish I was alone

Corpse

I drink your milk

Believe your lies

Feel your face

Against my thighs

You're so wise - your ilk

But dense like railroad ties

Eyes soaked with Mace

Still no time to cry

Your fuck is silk

And honest

Understanding his place

In history's eyes

So fuck the blame

I keep her inside

With all my shame

And formaldehyde

It ain't time to go soft

Not time to die

My heart held aloft

A kind prostitute's lies

It's poison, this life

None will survive

The pain and the strife

That they harbor inside

Embattled

The sadness hung above us like the clouds

Hand in hand, white knuckled in our defence

We could not speak our grievances aloud

We never had before and never sin(ce)

A fortune of past and future woes

Out to play in the moonlight for the eve

A battle of soundless strikes and blows

And afterwards for none to grieve

1982

The Gallup is real

It's the horse that's fake

But keep your chin up for goddamned God's sake

Put in the coin

And the bed would quake

If this were a motel

In 1982

Don't Go

She turned on the dish machine with a cough

We just took a smoke break in the alley

She knew me before, but we just really met

In this broken-down kitchen in this cold, wet valley

This is real life

We can do what we want

Remember Mr Fife?

Ha ha ha ha ha ha

What a loser he was

God he smelled like the fruit

Trapped in the dead kid's locker

Work

Tell me your dreams

Tell me your stories

Yes I like your voice

Yes I will read your poetry

It's all we can do today

It's almost time to close

Fuck the customers

What are we doing later?

Idaho

Don't go to Idaho

You can go anywhere

But don't go to Idaho

I heard there's dragons there

I'm just your friend I know

But the way I feel ain't fair

So don't go to Idaho

Because I'm not there

I'm here

Why did you leave that night?

What did I say?

It was fine until you asked

Why I looked at you that way

But I didn't answer

I just coughed

I didn't know what to say,

I just blew you off

You think you know my space

You think you can read my pauses

Like the lady at Brookdale Mall

I didn't mean that I loved you

I didn't mean I couldn't live without you

We are just good friends

If anything I see possibility

It's just a thing I think

It's not a reason to run from me

It's not a reason to shun me

It's not a reason to go

Don't go to Idaho

You can go anywhere

But don't go to Idaho

I heard they ride wagons there

I'm just your friend I know

But the way I feel ain't fair

So don't go to Idaho

Because I'm not there

I'm here

Here I will stay

You'll go away

I'll sweat and swear

I'll smoke all day

I won't go to Idaho

It's just not for me

I can't go to Idaho

It's just too far away

And what would you say?

If I just showed up one day

In the kitchen

By the dish machine?

Would you smile at me?

Would you run away?

I can't go

And neither should you

Idaho it's not for me and you

Stay away from me

This cannot be your place to be

Dear Chump,

Dear Chump,

You're too real to reel

I say fish potatoes mamma

I'll wallow if I wanna

The world can watch me heal

While they pump up their tennis shoes

But now I miss my shadow

I'm a ghost of a herd of cattle

I'm a baby with no rattle

A snake

Don't follow me home

About you was not the poem

I'm not the Prince of Rome

This at least I've shown

Stay away from us

It's nicer under the bus

Stay away from us

We were born to rust

Stay away from me

This is my fantasy

You'll just fuck it up

Nothing gonna break me

Nothing without weight at least

Shadow's need no air, you see

It ain't like me

I ain't even free

Yet

Love,

Ed

The Lost Singer

She's singing to the walls

Singing an empty song

But she's singing it beautifully

She's singing it perfectly

A voice like water falls

She can't do nothin wrong

She's not even here with me

Replaced by melancholy

Oh, I know that

She's as sick as me

But she doesn't know

So who'd you rather be?

Oh, I know

Ain't no recovery

Her mind is truly blown

Still, who'd you rather be?

She's singing to the walls

But there are no words

Still she's singing angelically

Like some ancient plea

Can't escape the walls

It doesn't matter what you've heard

It doesn't matter what you think

Let's go get another drink

Hiding

I can't give myself to you

Can't even breathe it true

What used to make me blue

Now breaks me apart

It can't be about the listening

The blinding resume glistening

I crossed the street from the picketing

Because I had to fart

It's a wild ecstatic hotel

Far from the deranged motel

On me to Mom you can go tell

But It'll break her heart

You Are Me

You are me if you wanna be

But I'm feeling the love of the dog in you

If we can ignore the crashing waves

It is just a phrase that I'm going through

I like to see things come together

I like to watch them fall apart

My mind and body may seem untethered

To your unconventional heart

And if you trust the weather

You may not even start

The Dance Floor

The music's blaring

Drowning out your over sharing

But still they're staring

It feels overbearing

But you're sick of caring

Why not do something daring?

You look at what you're wearing

Are they questioning the pairing?

You're dressed like a man waiting

Destined for masturbating

The music becomes more grating

That's your ego heard deflating

Because the one that you're dating

Is out there confiscating

Every eye on the dance floor

Every Hater in Their Hating

Fuck the dream I'm chasing

The pressure it is placing

On my heart I'm bracing

For a blow from he I'm face ing-

Grateful is pacing

Out the door with their new plaything

A Spanish fly racing

A poem of words we're wasting

Blessed

Heart barren, repressed, a magic incest –

uous tryst with my aunt and we soiled her dress

We had thought we were blessed

But we made such a mess

It was time to confess

But now our dicks they sting

Oh God on the cross

What had happened here?

Cruci-fix my thoughts

Let me not die right here

Rotten

They believe so entirely in spiritual absolution

They went and forgot that all acts of prostitution

Start and stop with a little protrusion

But wizards don't exist in this world of confusion

A blizzard of sexist acts blurred for amusement

Fuck their tired stretched out necromancy

Their visions of God and their fancy

Ideals and their unsexy dancing

Fuck their prancing

And crying

Their selfishness

They're lying

For these rotten fucks

Death's an enhancement

TV

I woke up early

the light through the window shocked my face

I took my dog

For a long cold walk to her favourite place

It's just what I do

To make myself feel better

And when I was younger

I thought there'd be an end

To the pain

It never ends

It just keeps on going and going

Like the ocean and the sky

It just keeps floating and blowing

If you feel tortured now

You'll feel tortured then

And when I watch TV

Or when I read on my phone

I'm so disappointed

In me

It's all my fault

It's on me

The dumb TV

Uninspired me

It's not gonna change

It's gotta feel broken

There's really no reason for you to try

Don't do anything

Don't stop

Don't start

Don't breathe

Invisible

Don't nobody know where I'm from

Nowhere

Don't nobody know who I am

No one

Don't nobody know what I do

Nothing

I got nothing left with you

My time is done

Duality

Big changes are what drive us

Make us whole

Living on a different clock

Like time is an enemy

To be bested

Leaving

No regrets

Only a wake that shakes the moored boats

Making "captains" wonder aloud

"What was that speeding mayhem?"

"Was that the incarnation of every restless dead soul?"

Find and enter an unknown chasm

Unfrightened by the heaving darkness

Flex and sweat and swoon and writhe

A wild animal convinced

That our thrashing

Will not only shake the cage

But open it

Freeing us

And those who witness the escape

Create new blood from old

Vomit truth

Weep with pride at the sadness

Flourish in failures

We cannot be broken, tamed, or forgotten

Fleshy, but with luminous souls

Shining a light only seen by the Gods

Or maybe

We are the light itself from which the gods began?

We are also

A puzzle

Solved

Returned to the box

Later reopened

Rebroken

Completed again

Doomed to repeat

It is a soft and easy world

It just feels hard

It Could Have Been Our Song

Standing on the kerb

Headphone-toting nerd

Give off the vibe that I am

Better off alone

Broken from the herd

Desperate begging to be heard

But my words are silence

Heard only as a moan

Tired of rolling out

The same old tired lines

I know what I'm about

Since I "heard the loud bassoon"

Bulging brains will burst

Straining gravy through a shirt

Sleeping through this curse

For the remedy's unknown

Driving my own hearse

As they throw rice and flowers

Checking through my purse

For anything I own

Cataclysmic dream

Changes my reality

Created memories all obscene

So I memorised the tome

Tore an ass hole in my pants

So I abandon all my plans

To ask her for a dance

This is my favorite song

Sign on the Wall

A world full of art

Everywhere for us to see

So we shackled it with industry

To conquer the boredom

Which gets replaced with apathy

Or nasty plastic surgery

So we can attract

What we always had before

(He pulled me off a bar stool

Because I called his ma a whore)

But with you it's strange

The truth seems easy

Though it comes out fat

Sweating

Wheezy

You have gifts that I hoped were mine

Once in fifteen times that I gave up wine

But it was the last time

For now

Please Little Poem

The day's end draws nearer

And we're feeling tired

No inspiration upon us

When the light expires

The dusk passes as well

Of nothing to speak

I pray to the night

To bring me not beneath

Just that one little poem

Come to me, come to me

Please little poem

Come to me

Happy

It's respect I desire

But I only get pity

It's crazy to expect

Eye contact in the city

I'm a horse with three legs

Tough, Haggard, and gritty

I'm sick like a dog

I feel fucking shitty

But there's life here

It's green, magical-pretty

It makes little sense

I guess I'm that petty

But here we are

We try to be happy

Broken-Hearted

He told me that life was just a numbers game

But he said it with so much disdain

That I doubted the strength of his conviction

I told him my favorite writers are just my friends

And we'll trade our diapers for Depends

One day and that's just fine with us

He looked at me confused and rudely dumped

A rack of dice into a Chihuly vase

Which he purchased easily with his performative funds

I pantomimed winding a watch

Where I only had a bare swath of skin

I hoped for him that we would find our peace

But he knew as well as I

That we'll know much more before we die

And most decisions come down to intuition

I opened a book of poems

I read him one by my friend Greig

He faked a gag and rolled his eyes

To the back of his head

Sayings are just a turn of phrase

But if I dropped you off in a maze

I know that you'd never find your way

I wondered hard and searched my mind

But never did I even find

Any reason why you'd need to

I parted ways with my new enemy

Feeling glassy-eyed and stuffed plenty

I ran till I sweat and found my way home

And now here I sit, broken-hearted

I finished the poem that I just started

I called Greig

Read it to him

And he laughed

Maybe Tomorrow/Elisa Brown

Maybe tomorrow

I'll learn how to make it work

It won't be so fake

I won't go berserk

Maybe tomorrow

I'll find my way back

To where I feel like I'm going

Maybe tomorrow

The light that shines from me

Will meet with the darkness inside

 Maybe tomorrow

The light will win for once

If I put my Saturdays in a bucket

And filled it up with rain

I'd be drowning by Sunday

On Monday start again

A week means less than nothing

And the years drive us insane

The choirs were singing

The church bells were ringing

I spent Sunday above ground

I set the steeples on fire

Frothing wanton desire

For young Elisa Brown

She'd left me a pauper

For all the foie gras I'd bought her

She giggled as they buried me down

It was just a slip of paper

Marked hard with an eraser

Stuffed into the only mailbox in our town

A handwritten deed stained with pork pie and mead

Signing over the rights to Miss Brown

Granddaddy's farm

Signed over to Elisa

She never loved a man less than me

Granddaddy's farm

It should long provide her

With moneys for her habits of blissful loveless greed

Granddaddy's farm

Quaint country charm

Steeped in family history

Signed it away to a girl that I'd paid

To keep me warm and lonely

The Verse

Pine needles fall on the soft ground

It sounds hollow under your feet

Your mind races nowhere while your breath catches up

Your thoughts are a million years deep

It's a dangerous song that's stuck in your head

A dangerous verse tumbles 'round

Beware the harsh lyrics from which you can't break free

Just think of something pretty instead

There's a mountain of poems about the trees and the streams

And the cottages in the woods in the snow

There's so many songs about the white dove's flight

Or the majesty of nature's reverent flow

But your mind is hijacked by these lowlife verses

They're dark and vile, and violent

You scavenge about for a thing better to repeat

But on this your thoughts are silent

Let it flow over like a charging mad river

Let it thrash and roar like a storm

The control you seek of your mind is fruitless

like wishing you were never yet born

It's there for a reason, respect it

Life is not just sunshine and young dogs

You'll find upon examination

That despite your hesitation

Gravity had been here all along

Dear Irene,

I promise I'm fine

You don't have to call my work this time

I don't even work on Wednesdays

Why don't you call your friend Steve?

You know what I can't believe?

That what we don't fear just goes away

Like, I'm not afraid of dying so I'm not gonna die

And I'm not afraid of flying so I'm not gonna fly

And I'm not afraid of being with you

So what should we do?

Ed

Dear Irene, Part 2

Your portion size is off the plate

But that's not why this is our fate

I don't want to go to the buffet later

That place only fills my remorse

You say you could eat a horse

But there's leftovers in the refrigerator

You know I'm not afraid of pain so don't nothing hurt

I'm not afraid of you leaving so go ahead and call Kurt

I'm not afraid of this ending but it ain't over yet

Oh, wait

Yeah, it is

Ed

Good Enough

Hey Momma

Hey Pops

I broke into the house

And someone called the cops

Now I'm shaking here wild-eyed

Fearlessly petrified

I'm waiting for the rising tide

Of shame to wreck me down

And I know I ain't like you

I came out a little rough

I coulda been better

But I been good enough

Good enough for my friends

Good enough for the night

Good enough for misanthropes

That gave me a chance

Good enough for a night's sleep

Free of these thoughts

Good enough to ask Cindy Lou

Out for a dance

And what's so great about you?

You ain't that tough

Sure I coulda been refineder

But I'm fancy enough

Good enough for my friends

That smoke in the park

After going out drinking

With the commoners in the dark

They are ruins of the evening

And they are falling apart

But they're real as a last meal

And that's a good start

So hey Momma

Hey Pops

The sirens approaching

Did suddenly stop

Something just happened

Ain't that a bitch?

And here I just woke

In this godful ditch

I'm good enough, Momma

I'm good enough Pops

And if you don't see it

You may call the cops

And You're good enough, too

And you know I love you

But I ain't sorry

For living my way

Impressions

I just lay there

In the grass

Watching the blades

Sweetly move

With the wind

And the light

Gently reflecting

In infinite directions

A truck rumbles by

And the weight

Of the world

Remembers me

I close my eyes

Push myself up

And walk away

Only to look back

And see the impression

Of my body

In the grass

Will You?

If I write a poem

And share it with you

Will you show your friends?

Will they like it too?

Could they find it strange?

So what if they do?

My pen couldn't know

What thoughts might ensue

I can't help but share

All my thoughts with you

And just in case I

Fall in to a well

And I'm never found

I want you to tell

Everyone you know

There are no poets in hell

'Cept the one you knew

For which fate befell

With his tortured soul

And you knew him well

But that can't happen

I know I won't die

Because my words are

Dancing down your spine

With feet so hot

They set a line of fires

And you know how I

I can't help but lie

I just want a small

Slice of apple pie

And not to die

Time

The poetry of the grind

The clock be my aim

Tick tick as it goes

As my time falls away

My Bike

What good is the money if there's nobody to spend it on

The good guitar with nobody to play it with

What good is the life built for the future if the future is
bleeding out the past

The target is an empty hole

A hungry cavern, a bottomless stomach of an angry dragon

I am consumed by it

The future has already eaten me

But my bike

When I get on my bike

On my way to a job that eats everything I love about life

I feel myself rush back in

I feel myself

I live for half an hour

I then I walk in the door

And die

Until I ride home

I live for an hour a day

Throwing Bottles at the Trains

I was sitting on a bluff

Throwing bottles at the trains

I've always had enough

When it comes to flesh and brains

The wind it bites my ears

And my fears they fill my eyes

All the lies I told

You tried to tell them back to me

I ain't lost because

I was never going anywhere

I was just setting there

Throwing bottles at the train

I ain't fine anymore

I thought you were gone

I waited so long

For you to get here

Friends

And now

The crash

It falls

With a splash

And a man

With a hat

And a bushy

Mustache

He asked

Where I'm at

"I'm right here

"Why do you ask?

He laughed

I snapped

A friend once told me

That friends are transitory

When he left I wondered

If he would ever come back

Closed Doors and Tattered Window Dressings

The streets had been dry for months

When it rained that Saturday

His wet hair fell out in clumps

What does that matter

For they had forgotten him

And now he's just lost, unconscious

He went home last Thanksgiving

To closed doors and tattered window dressings

He coughed and remembered the smell

Of his Mom's cornbread stuffing

She didn't bake it in the bird

The bar down on Gables Lane

And 5th Avenue South

It smelled like a stable

But they were open on every holiday

It isn't so sad as it sounds

That he went home last Thanksgiving

To closed doors and tattered window dressings

Looked through a broken window

Remembered getting taught

He was never spared the belt

The jeans he wears are threadbare

From that old wooden chair

He's got all he's got in his pockets

And the rain is soaking through

Next Thanksgiving he'll just stay here

Behind the door of his hotel room

Maybe he'll call some company

Staying dry for the wettest reasons

The Stairs

We are so far away from home that it feels like outer space

We know just how to be scared, broken glass, can of mace

Forgetting what it means to be you and me anymore

I'm not rich now, but I still kinda miss being poor

We were formerly a happy pair, you know?

Then you threw me down the stairs, you know?

You thought I was an intruder, I think

I'm in a database on the computer, I think

The Rain

The rain will stop

Though it might take months

I'll be at the bus stop

For hours just waiting

The rain washes away

Everything it touches

All the loam and sand and clay

And then it replaces it

The rain is a blue background

To my winter life here

It's dripping off the swingset

I still remember

Everything

Faces

It's crowded in here

All the faces look forward and down

I look at them and they look away

I try to guess their identity

How much time do they spend on their hair?

Clothes?

Shoes?

How big are their headphones?

How small?

We're inside together

Why the sunglasses?

For shame?

For pride?

She really loves that dog

The dog seems indifferent

Indifference is a great identity

It matches everything

Every person

Every season

Every outfit

That dog could rule the world

She doesn't seem to know

Brimless hat

Head scarf

So many necklaces

Blue hair

A squeaky toy on your bike

Unicorn tattoo

Cleavage

Mullet

Sports team

Yell and scream

We're not aware of you quite yet

We don't understand

You're right

We won't try

The loudest are never heard

And they shouldn't be

The Last Sleep

Did you choose to fight?

Did the fight find you?

Are you happier bloodied?

I won't let you take away

What I earned

Deserved

These wings

That never knew flight

Or even felt the wind

Too crooked to be real

And too sad to be fake

When you lay your head down

For the last time

And you know it will be the last time

Will you be able to fall asleep?

You won't

You'll lay awake

Wondering

Thinking

About every friend you failed

About every ex-lover

About your dog

Who will they all love now?

After your last sleep?

Every sound and smell will be magnified

Berating your senses

You won't rest before you go

Because you didn't really live

Instead

You just lay there

Wondering

Thinking

Your entire life

And you only loved as much as you could

Which wasn't much at all

And you never chose to fight

And no fights chose you

So you can't sleep now

Before your last sleep

Because you never were awake

The Flower in the Fragile Breeze

Why do anything?

Why would anyone read poetry

When we have so many things to do?

On demand videos

Of personal injury

And bursting pustules

And athletic people

Having sex

With other athletic people

Because they weren't athletic enough

To be athletes

Animals being saved to feel good

Animals being abused to feel bad

Or superior

So much to make you feel superior

Idiots espousing views that they don't understand

Feeling like geniuses because the camera

Is pointed at them

But they pointed the camera

And then there is work

And school

Or education

Depending on which you choose

And time with family

And friends

And friends of friends

Family of friends

Friends of family

All eating your attention

Clogging up your stories

Your history

While you don't read poetry?

Who has the time?

Between shifts

And meetings

And appointments

With people who don't respect you

Or listen to you

Who make you wonder why you are even there

In the meeting

But you need to get paid

So you can clothe and feed yourself

And be

An upstanding

Member

Of

Society

Not

A

Hungry

Naked

Schlub

Wasting time

Hopeless

Without meaningful goals

What a terrible use of time

Reading poetry

About the way the light looks

When it screams through the trees

Or the fog

At the break of dawn

And makes you feel so

Fucking

Alive

You can smell it in your sleep

Because that's where you are

At daybreak

Sleeping

Or getting ready

To do something

Anything

Worthwhile

Make money

Buying

Living life

Keeping the boss off your back

You don't have to be faster than the bear

They say

Who has the time?

To read poetry?

Or anything else

For

That

Matter

Or to write it?

For

God's

Sake

Stop

God's is the language of commerce

Unconcerned

With the itching eyes

Bleeding with guilt

For what you saw

Yourself do

With your own

White innocent

Supple hands

Nothing you love

It's worth doing

You can't make any money

Doing things

Like that

You

Have

To

Do

Anything

Else

Grow up

It's time

You are as much a poet

As you are a flower

Delicately swaying

In the fragile breeze

On a cliff-side

That no human has ever seen

So cut it out

Our Song

I think I hate this song

It's been stuck in my head all day long

I wrote it back when we used to get along

Back when our love was strong

We'd pretend we were Louis Armstrong

I loved your fake gravelly voice

We were young and we made a lotta noise

At least 10,000 sex toys

Keeping those neighbors up as if they had a choice

Happily unemployed

It was the 90s back in Illinois

I never thought that you would fall for other boys

I didn't know you even looked at other boys

We used to laugh until our eyes fell out

And you know I never had a doubt

That I could pick you from a crowd

After all these years rolled out

I'm laughing until I'm crying at the road

And this story is almost told

Because I'm not getting old

I'm there - it happens quick like mould

A wild bouquet of marigolds

My heart an exhausted manifold

And that's why I hate this song

It broke us apart with no time to string along

I thought that we were strong

So, my dear, so long

I knew this was coming all along

Please return my bong

And my favourite pair of tongs

Goodbye and thank you for the song

Ill Fitting Pants

You did that little dance

When you jumped out into traffic

It was so extravagant

What's it like to be so manic?

You didn't need that second helping

I'm with that girl whose yelping

We do what we do

You did what you did

I don't judge you for it

You're crazy

I've known you all my life

But I'm meeting you just now

You had that old, trashed jacket

And your ill-fitting men's pants

Your eyes were both soft and erratic

Nobody ever stood a chance

All life is bereft of balance

A red cup can be a chalice

You do what you do

And we did what we did

I can't forget it

You're amazing

I've known you all my life

But I'm meeting you just now

You're amazing

I've known you all my life

But I'm meeting you just now

There's nothing wrong with us

We can't solve on the bus

I've known you all my life

But I'm meeting you just now

You're amazing

I've known you all my life

But I'm meeting you just now

Knotty Pine

About a mile away there's a park that we never visit

There's this old knotty tree with sparse leaves

The times we've gone you just sat there and stared at it

Back then I would have rather not gone anywhere

Now that your gone I'm at that park everyday

I look at your tree and I can't look away

And I wish that I'd wanted to go there with you

Coffee

I felt like I should have been able to smell coffee

There were two polite police at the screen door

I heard the words shouted "back up off me!"

I swear that I've never heard that voice before

When the nightmares are all you have left

To get you through the short days

In your youth you dreamed of a castle out west

You believed you had something to say

Now a maid and a hooker could replace you

They might do a much better job

Your mind thoughtfully rendered like horse glue

You'd be better off as a blob

Is it too late for trying?

I'm as busy living as I am dying

You might recognize my wailing

I'm sure it's too late for trying

If you said it weren't I'd say "stop lying."

A billion dead cats outside crying

I Ain't Thin

I felt like the man who's inside me

The struggle is only deceit

The crying is only a catastrophe

Because it occurred to me in the street

I ain't no criminal but I done a lot wrong

I'll try to tell you about it in the song

This ain't no confessional

You ain't no priest

And this ain't the truth

There's a few lies at least

I got no time for regrets

Remorse is a friend of mine

Fuck it I did what I done

Mostly to waste the time

I ain't thin I ain't thick

I ain't lost just not found

And I don't want to live

With my head stuck in the ground

The Cool Breeze

You have only one day left

To swing your junk in the breeze

So swing it

With vigour

And proudly

And please

Don't fret

About your nudity

Even They won't judge

The dying

And if you live on

For days

Weeks

Years

Remember that feeling

Of freedom

The blue

Sky

Burning

High through white clouds

The smell of grass clippings

And diesel

And forget

If you will

The worry

You fought

Forget

Looking for eyes

In the distance

Forget my young friend

That you knew you would die

That you beat it

This time

Means nothing

Anything

I'll do anything

I'll leap

From the bridge

Into cold

Cold

Waters

But I won't listen to you

I won't be taught

By you

I know

And you know

You have nothing

Of value

For me

I'll suffer

Through

The worst

Of it

The beautiful tortures

Life gives

And I'll enjoy it

More than

Listening to you

Tell me how to live

How to go about

My life

And telling me

What should be

How

To

Succeed

I can see your doubt

It's draped over you

Like a wet white sheet

Translucent

And cold

And you

Have the balls

To pretend

To me

That you know

What is best

I may be uncommon

I may be full

Overflowing

With

Tumult

Pain

Sadness

Regret

Addiction

Angst

All of it

But I'm not up there

Pretending

I have the answers

To what you should do

I'll take a

Sword

To the heart

Before I hear

A single word

Of your poisonous

Advisement

And you wonder

Why I don't raise

My hand

They seem so smart

You think

But no motivation

You think

So sad

You think

And I think

You are

Even more

Deranged

Delusional

Depressed

Than I

And worse

You believe the

Programming

That tells you

You are right

And righteous

And good

Despite

The

Evidence

Contrary

The classless rubric

Entices the dull

To get angry

And spew forth

The violent words

They're repeating

Repeater

The people I met plagued with indecision

They think 20 times before they make an incision

They prefer not to go through any transition

The nerves pile up and their brain disturbs them

But me I fear any kind of stagnation

When I write the words come like mad confusion

I promise I have no contusion

I'm just not comfortable with repetition

And I'm just not comfortable with repetition

No I'm just not comfortable with repetition

I'm just not comfortable

I'm just not comfortable

I'm just not comfortable with repetition

And you might think that to take an action

Or wonder how it will get any traction

If you throw your hands in the air to cause a distraction

You prefer solitude because you know how to act then

Tardigrade Parents

We fried up some eggs in the ecotone

Drank plum wine at the demilitarized zone

If I can't see you in person I'll call you on the phone

He orders a sandwich and expects a T-bone

Serve me up a riff on the Casio-tone

Many things are worse than being alone

Every banana you eat is made from a clone

Of all the songs we sang twas the short ones who shone

A tardigrade got no meat and no bones

But listen to those motherfuckers play the trombone

Mom, do you think that I can get really rich?

Writing poetry and drinking in a ditch

Every time I fuck my feet really itch

I used to work with a deaf guy named Ed Begenestitch

I'm going to the store but I'm not taking a list

Since I got no feet I'm getting off the pitch

If there's a wrinkle in time it seems like a glitch

Better get some little statues to make your boat house kitsch

Remember old Jay kissed that bitch with a lisp

Now he's down in Joliet on a six-year stretch

Please, please tromboner, go on, we insist

Dad, do you think about heaven and hell?

My blanket's on the street but I got nothing to sell

I feel like a rowboat stuck on a 40-foot swell

But if I'm frightened there ain't not a soul that could tell

Not a hair outta place on account of the gel

You know my friends, you hated, then tragedy befell

One after the other wait in a cell for a lunch bell

But we ain't mad and each one of them wishes you well

And we all still prefer magics to morels

Not morals, though we got 'em, but on that I won't dwell

I'm just here to say good-bye, then back to the brothel

I Understand

My mind is not afraid

To travel to where it's never been

To break apart

And come back together again

Never knowing

If it ever will

My mind is not afraid

But I understand that yours is

It's natural and practical

To assume that madness

Is an unpleasant destination

And sure,

I wouldn't want to live there

But to go there for a break

Just a whimsical turn of phrase

As an excuse

For the way I behave

I like to think it's

Bold, courageous, and brave

My mind is not afraid

To offend you

Or your sensibilities

And neither am I

He who I knew

Who I was before

Can stay trapped, screaming

Behind the thick glass door

Crying, waiting

Between broken sandy shores

Naked, mashed, thoughtless, confused, scared, shifting, crawling, gnawing

See me mommy

I'm trying

I'm sorry

You must have known I was trying

He who I knew I was before

Is afraid to show his face here

He stays where he is

And the glass grows thicker

Obscuring and magnifying

The best and the worst

Of his awful magnificence

I'm only sorry

For those he hurt

And if I'm honest

Not even them

Maybe

Especially not them

Prison

There's only so many chords

I know just how they live together

And there are so many words to sing

But they're not all clever

And when it comes to gifts

It's when you choose to give 'em

Bake me a cake with a shiv

And deliver it to my prison

The salt in my eyes

The grit in my teeth

The grease in my hair

The world at my feet

The fork at my tongue

The wild in my heart

Fuck Joan of Arc

And Napoleon Bonaparte

The Bar and the Leaf

I never found a way to town that

Didn't go past the bar

And I never found a way to get back that

Didn't go too far

But don't tell me I went the wrong way

It just ain't the way you went

Look at that last leaf on the tree

It should not be here it's winter

It'll get pushed out in the spring

Nothing can hang on forever

The bent old trellis soaked in brown dust

And a single black leaf that don't know that it's dead

But dead or dying it's still hanging on

Dead or dying, I'm still hanging on

Why should I rot on the ground with the rest of my friends?

It will take a helluva wind to break me

My softness gives me strength

You find that ironic

But I know it makes sense

We Are Bound

It's like time didn't pass for her

She was geologic, organic, and eternal

I never thought she could be anything other

I didn't know she was sadistic

I couldn't hold her far from my heart

My fucking sad, angry mystic

And she spoke in music

And also when she screamed

Each footprint was poetry

And now she shuffles

And now she grumbles

And now she startles

At every sound I make

Like she forgets I'm here

And sometimes

If I'm honest

So, do I

And what about you?

Did you know her when she was hyperbolic?

When she could bend a supernova?

With just a look

With just a nod

With just a smile

It's a pity that we all will crumble

But without that what would we have?

We're not trees

Stuck in the mud

Never knowing

That we are

What we are

If that is even knowable

Inflatable

Like my ego and my id

On vacation

Like a raisin

A grape left in the sun to wrinkle

And there she goes

Just shuffling and grumbling away

Grinding down Mill Street

Towards the old house where she used to stay

The people there just hope she'll go away

And like me and you she'll just die someday

And they'll rejoice

Secretly

And in a wooden box she'll go to sleep

The earth

Has no memory

It doesn't think of you and me

Or her

Though it should

For she could turn mountains into

Blood

Blood to wine

Sure, yeah, why not?

She was all the stars at once

At least to me

I know I'm not free

I'm in a cage

Caught in a trap

Tied myself tight to the railroad tracks

What Castle?

I don't know where you're going, do you?

I've never met a man who spoke the truth.

My girl painted the doghouse blue

And she told me where to sleep

But it's all right the air is calming

Anyway, she's still my darling

To me she is a bit more charming

When I am outside piled in a heap

If your goal is to build a castle

Before your dead and gone

You best get all you need

But if that all seems a hassle

And you carry all you want

Collect thee nothing and godspeed

The job was a burden, the boss worse

Watch me as I stuff my purse

I hope to remember my ride in the hearse

As I am cold and lowered

You'll forgive me for my lack of success

And for my unpleasant dress

I wrote this out knowing it won't impress

But the joy it brought me stands proudly

If your goal is to build a castle

Before your dead and gone

You best get all you need

But if that all seems a hassle

And you carry all you want

Collect thee nothing and godspeed

I know exactly what I could have been

Maybe rich, and powerful, like the great men

Or famous, revered, instead of forgotten

How comfortable I am with my choices

Empires crumble at the hands of the great

And they are built, call it all fate

I got fired again because I was late

And I can't give half a damn

If your goal is to build a castle

Before your dead and gone

You best get all you need

But if that all seems a hassle

And you carry all you want

Collect thee nothing and godspeed

We are we who don't need your approval

And we are much more than alright

Our lives to you are not crucial

If not entirely blight

Fuck it, I scream from the top of the cliff

Where you intend to build

I feel safe now and will the day I turn stiff

So fuck you, your ilk, and your guild

Fake Flowers in a Pitch-Black Room

Go ahead and plant those Fake Flowers

In your pitch-black room

You're soft, still, and pale

Pour fake water

Into the plastic pot

Just to go through the steps

Of being human

Your eyes can adjust to darkness

Because in darkness there's light

But in this pitch-black room

The only adjustments

Are in your mind

Let's pretend that they aren't fake flowers at all

Maybe they're fake tomatoes

Fake potatoes

Or fake rice

You could never die in the blackness

With so much to

Pretend to eat

And maybe you're not pale at all

Perhaps you are also green

Or pink and purple and patchy

Who's fantasy is this?

And why are you in it?

It's depressing

And it makes me mad

Let me out of here

Let me see

Let me smell

Let me taste before I go

I deserve that

Even if

I didn't before

Even if

I don't deserve you

I can move on

Move forward

Even snakes and mice do

Fall Apart

Why should it be so hard to still an aching heart

The cold air met the engine, and it wouldn't start

A wild-minded child you must do your best to tame

The low storm coming bringing the smell of death in rain

Did you say, dear one, that you remember what I taught?

Or did you just memorize the words

I lay here, I am dying, and all my life was naught

The whole thing is so absurd

So absurd

The fire blazing in the hearth it is not there

It's an old empty house which from the windows I stare

The cars keep driving by, can they feel what I feel

Are there even drivers in them - are the drivers real

A broken line of poetry is written on the wall

With soot from the ashes of a fire

I'm broken from just one line - good I didn't read it all

The author must have been a good liar

The building is leaning against the ground

which is writhing up into the air

The operator makes that sound

A gurgling dry despair

Fall apart

You were never broken

Fall apart

You were never broken

It's your turn

It's your turn

That Explains It

Gotta bullet in my spine makes me walk a little funny

Gotta healthy cocaine habit makes my nose a little runny

Dear Layla,

It's been years since we last spoke

The rain fell off the leaves that night

And it drenched us both

I screamed at you, so violent

I waited for you to scream back

But you stood there, so silent

Like you were under attack

And I cried, I wailed,

I asked you to make it stop

But that ship had sailed

The life that we had for naught

I'm not sorry

I'm not sure

What could I even say

I was just so insecure

So young and far away

I'm not sure of this feeling

It could be just regret

You're in my head and reeling

Like a mental silhouette

Landlord

My fat fucking pig fucking landlord

Just raised my rent again

For my shitty ass tiny apartment

A negative 26 out of ten

So I guess I'm gonna move

To some other fucked up place

Even if it costs a little more

Fuck his fat ass face

Vultures and pigs

Assholes and thugs

Meet Me

There were some people that battered my youth

It hurt me much more than I let on

To tell the truth

But I grew strong

I fought, and fuck them, anyway

I can't let them take my youth from me here while I age

Maybe one day I'll find you in the light

There, where there's no room for sadness or fright

I am so tired now

I'm not down

I've got some time left

And in true

The darkest thoughts

Feel like all I have left

But I fight

Like I fought before

And I'll keep on and on

Until I'm bloodied and more

If I die

Sing a song for me

And cry if you must

But remember, that I lived enough to make a powerful dust

And you can throw it in the eyes of your enemies

As you keep on and on with the good fight

Darling, goodnight

Fall

Fate dies and dreams

When you're thinking about nothing

You know what he meant

He said it over and over

"Oh, I'll find the time to heal someday

I'll sleep when I'm dead

I'm too stubborn for therapy

Dogs are better than people"

The smoke from his hands

He breathed out cold fire

I was stuck in the back

Of that hot car forever

The world has fallen

Is what they always think

But it's fine it's as it should be

It changes like a river roams

"Oh, I'll find the time to heal someday

I'll sleep when I'm dead

I'm too stubborn for therapy

Keep your hands off my car"

Hold me, my dear

No, I didn't need to cry

I just want to be still

For a minute or two

I was stuck

Now I'm free

For this I thank you

If there's time I think we

Should go get a beer

"Oh, I'll find the time to heal someday

I'll sleep when I'm dead

I'm too stubborn for therapy

Carlin was always right"

I like fall more than winter

Prefer dying over death

Just don't ask me to write down

My thoughts in your notebook

The Dong of Our Lord

Click, click, click

Tsk, tsk, tsk

Clipity clop, clop, clop

Goes the broken, judgemental clock

It runs backwards sometimes

As lava pours from its breast

8,679

Days have passed

But the laundry never got done

And mother was disappointed

A million miles is far too far to run

With sheets so semen anointed

If you must know, Lenore

I'm not a monster anymore

I'm still so fucking poor

That I can't attend the zoo

And for the record, Lenore

It doesn't make you a bore

In the sack to be less hardcore

And refrain from smearing your poop

And where did you learn that, anyway?

Did you attend prison in Spain?

Where in the cities it rains

Piss when they run out of gloop?

Slop, slop, slop

Splat, splat, splat

Rock hard cock

Desiring much more than a crusty sock

That is standing up straight like a statue

On the bedside table of God

Who in addition to omnipresence

Also has a magnificent rod

Mirror Lake

Fuck the rest

Fuck the feelings in you

Fuck the musings of others

Fuck what could be better

Fuck the mirror

It's just painted glass

Water does the same thing in a still lake

It does it better

It reflects truer

Because it's distorted

Wanderers

Not all who are lost are wandering

But some are

Some are all pondering the wonderment around them

Still others be blundering, fucking it up for the rest of us

I see you boss, fuck your test

I'd rather just take the bus to work

Than drive some damn Tesla or Honda

And now, am I lost

I am floundering

Buying powder to suck all up like Hoover or Knight Rider

So how's the wind blowing?

Is it feeling exciting?

Can you feel your heart beating in your chest?

It's all blood and rust

Can you hear it?

They're trying

Watching ads

Flying tanks

Chewing fat to fast

Stabbing their necks

With makeshift knives

It's either them or us

From the Top

It wants us dead

Or at least to suffer

We're suffering

Even the rich

And the good looking

Even the ones

Who pretend the best

We're not alone

Despite how it feels

We're all connected

Through shared exclusion

Shared delusion

Pardon the intrusion

Let's start at the top

I don't give a fuck

Where you're from or where you've been

You start at zero from the day we meet

I didn't give a fuck if you're a man or woman

Or any way you feel in between

I couldn't possibly care

Who you love or who you screw

How could that matter to me?

You can have your god

From the Buddha to JC

It's all good

It's all the same to me

If your daddy was a thief

Or the king or queen himself

If he was a pillar of industry

Be a woman

Be a man

Be a trans queer lesbian

Be on drugs

I don't know

Pray to God

Row a boat

Be damn rich

And damn poor

Be a priest

Be a whore

I won't show you the door

I'm not a hugger

So, I'll shake your hand

And congratulate you

On being you

Understand?

I only judge me

And I judge me harshly

I'm too busy to consider your plan

And if someone stands tall

And says you don't matter at all

Or that you should shame in who you are

I'll stand next to you

I'll fight till I'm blue

I have your back

And I'm not alone

The Day We Met

I never told a story in my life that wasn't true

'Cept for the one about the day that I met you

I tell a tale of how your beauty surpassed the sky's

But to tell the truth I was underestimating'

Your beauty eclipses a thousand skies

Above a million planets, reflected in a billion starlets eyes

And when I touch you my heart falls to pieces

And when I hold you the pieces explode

And those explosions become a symphony

And sound and light themselves would get on bended knee

To ask for your hand in marriage right away

They didn't know that only I can have you

I redefine lucky everyday

It hardly makes any sense

To say that I deserve you, my love

Is complete and utter nonsense

You outclass my shenanigans

The Rain

Never knew a month a Sundays

Every day's about the same

Never had no time for schoolin'

Cuz the teachers were so mean

"You won't amount to nothing"

That's what they'd say to me

"Won't go nowhere with that attitude"

"Well, I'll have to disagree"

The thoughts of other people

Are the noises in the clouds

They don't change anything

But they sure sound fucking loud

So fucking loud

Fuckin loud

But the rain, the rain is different

It's more like the thoughts in me

Rain can soak me, it can slow me down

It can cause catastrophe

I don't know many people

I got the friends I got

To be liked or loved or hated

Don't add up to diddly-squat

Go you pile up your winnings

Your materials and friends

I'll hold on to my worn-out few

To the broken bitter end

The musings of my restless mind

Come to rest beside a brook

If you stay for just one minute

You can't get quite unhooked

Can't get unhooked

Unhooked

The mirror in the water

It's better than a vanity

Truer because it's distorted

That anyone can see

Anyone can see

Can see

Anyone can see me

Down by the water

The water's staring back at me

Can't you see?

You can't look to me

For any answers

About being free

Cuz to be free

Takes struggle

To be free

Embrace that ambiguity

The thoughts of other people

Are the noises in the clouds

They don't really affect me

But they sound so fucking loud

So fucking loud

So loud

But the rain, the rain is different

It's more like the thoughts in me

Rain can soak me, slow me down

And it can set me free

Death Med

Please sit comfortably

You should be wearing loose clothing

Or no clothing at all

Try, if you can, to be totally at ease

Let you fear melt away and your vulnerability be complete

You can sit, lie down, stand on one foot

However you feel truly one with yourself

With your breath

If the room is cool or cold

Or warm or hot

Acknowledge that

But don't try to change the temperature

Accept it

Then realize that you are not truly comfortable

You never have been

Even weightlessness would be accompanied by discomfort

Breathe

Relish is your small discomforts

Breathe

Being connected to your breath is critical

Breath is our connection

To the earth

To the people around us

Breath is life

And life is breath

Breathe in a way that is comfortable

It can be in through the mouth or nose

Out through the mouth or nose

Whatever helps you

To clear your mind

Of all but breath

Clear your mind and just breathe

Then recognize the things you can't clear

The stresses

The chaos

The fear

The feelings of inadequacy

No mind can be clear

All minds work, run, race

Yours is no different

You are not special

No one is special

Relish your unquiet mind

Joy in your thoughts

But come back to your breath

And try to think only

"I am breathing"

Continue coming here as we move forward

Come to this place of acceptance

Not calm

Not controlled

Acceptance

When I say breathe

Take as long as you'd like to just breathe

Even if it means ignoring the words I am saying

I am unimportant

These words are unimportant

Relax your whole body

Each step of the way

As I list your body parts

Feel them awaken with your acknowledgement

As if called to action

The release them from duty

Picture them softening

Turning to liquid

And flowing out into the world

Relax your neck

The top of your head

Your back

Shoulders

Abdomen

Your bowels

Your arms

Your hands

Fingers

Legs

Toes

Your Ears

Your mouth

Your jaw

Close your eyes

Then release them from the need to focus

Unfocus inside your head

Let it all blur

Relax your genitals

Your anus

Your forehead

All these things are yours

More so than your home or your car

Because

When you are gone

They go with you

Finally, relax your mind

Relax your mind by accepting it

Don't worry if it continues to race

It is good

It is your mind

You know it best

Breathe

As you fall deeper into this state of breath and acceptance

Imagine you are in a wide green field on a spring day

Feel the tall grass under your feet

The breeze on your skin

Smell the smells of spring

The wetness

The light smell of diesel and death

Hear the distant birds

The wind

A distant oboe playing a sorrowful tune

You are walking

Barefooted

You feel soft soil

Squish between your toes

The sun warms you

Think again of your discomforts

Both in your current position

Resting and breathing

Eyes closed

Relaxed

And your imagined one

Walking through a warm field

Breathe

And enjoy your discomfort

The scratchy grass

The sound of bugs

You feel them on your skin

Let them be

Love them

Breathe

Adjust your position

Itch any itches

You are a complete success

You might be the best at meditation

There are no awards

And you are not

In your imaginary walk you come across a small pond

It beckons you

And you oblige

You enter the pond swiftly from a rickety wooden dock

It creaks as you step on it

And you jump in

Water rushing over your head

The water is cold

Enjoy the shock of cold

You notice that it is warmer the lower you swim into the
pond

You are curious

Your experience tells you that it should be warmer at the top

Your curiosity causes a thought

You would like to know the source of the warmth

So, you swim down further

And Further

Diving deeper and deeper into the pond

As you swim you realize that the pond is very, very deep

And it continues to get warmer

But it never gets hot

It is very pleasant

You calmly settle into the warmth

The water feels thicker here

Almost like a jelly

You enjoy breathing through the jelly

The breaths are warm and nourishing

All worry falls away

As you confidently breath weightlessly and warm in blue jelly

It heals and nourishes your lungs

Your beating heart

Your unquiet mind

Breath for 30 seconds now

Breath in the blue jelly

1, 2, 3, 4, 5… 13, 14, 15, 16… 27, 28, 29 and 30

As you finish counting

Your breath becomes more difficult

Laboured

It's as if the jelly is losing its power

It's stiffening like setting concrete

You open your eyes

And looking up you see the blue light of the sun

Your eyes burn

Not from the sun, but from the jelly

The burn there makes you suddenly aware

That you feel burning all over

Any open cuts burn

Your anus, ears, and urethra burn

The burning intensifies

And you close your eyes

You cannot take deep breaths

Just short gasps

But they seem to be enough for now

Looking around

Through distorted blue jelly

You cannot find an exit

Your breathing is becoming more laboured

You are panicking

The jelly is turning purple

You wonder if you are dying

You are not

But

You realize now

Gasping breaths of oxygenated jelly

That there is no escape

You are in a sealed glass cube

The glass is inches thick

But even if it wasn't

The jelly restricts your movement so much

And your strength is so diminished

That you couldn't break the glass

If it was bone China

Breathe

Breathe as much as you can

While you are still alive

It is difficult

But important to be aware that you are dying

Even if not today

Not in this cube

In this Jelly

Which is turning red

But you are

You have always been dying

Even before you knew what you were

If you do know

You relax into this state

If you are to survive at all today

Even in a changed form

Don't worry about the term "changed form"

It will all be okay

As long as you make it through this part

This is the worst part

Breathe

Let your relaxation deepen

Force relaxation

Remember what the field was like before you jumped in

Remember the breeze and the grass

Keep your eyes closed

Feel the burning all over

It has entered you, the burning

It burns your esophagus

Your lungs

Accept it

As you would accept the hug of a loved one

Or an attractive stranger

Imagine yourself naked with the stranger that you pictured

Even if it is not a stranger

It is all burning

Enjoy the burning

Relish the burning of life before it is extinguished

It's all red

Violent red

Think again of the field you were in

Just minutes ago

The light was warming your face

Relax

Concentrate

There is no escape

Your eyes adjust to the jelly

And the distorted red light

And you become aware that you are

Not alone

You are not in a pond at all

In fact

You are not anywhere you've ever seen

Or even imagined

And a figure is observing you

Through the glass

They appear pink and red

As if badly burned

Or perhaps

They never had any skin at all

They begin tapping at the glass

Tap, tap, tap

They have very long fingers

And bulbous knuckles

They have no fingernails

And their fingertips are purple and blue

Veiny

Tap, tap, tap

Close your eyes again

Try to calm yourself

To breathe

But you find that your eyes will no longer close

Nor can you close your mouth

You still feel the burning

But the terror you feel is distracting you from it

You notice that your anus has been opened

And your urethra expanded

As the jelly flows into you through every opening

It appears to be replacing your blood

Your body is swelling

You can see the ghoulish being more clearly now

It is communicating with you

They have two others with them

Each one is disturbingly unskinned

They are humming

Mouthless humming

A song you recognize

It is a song your mother sang to you

To put you to sleep

But tune is somehow discordant, and scary

You are going to die here

The thought invades your fragile mind

Or

Was it told to you?

It was told to you

All of these messages were

And always have been

And you can relax

Knowing that I

Have always been here

You only know the cube

You have no anus

No genitals

No mouth

You have nothing to relax

You are jelly in a cube

Not a cube

A bulb

A pod

You are here only for my observation

I created you

And

When I choose to

I will kill you

When I bore of hearing your thoughts

Your racing

Self-absorbed

Thoughts

But it is not today

Today I will let you go back you your waking world

The glass shatters

The beings disappear

I disappear

You open your eyes

Take a deep breath

It is time to go on with your day

Wasted on the Aging

I'm not young anymore

I still feel new to this world

I'm curious, and anxious, and strange

But when my skin was smoother and my gait was cleaner

I had a confidence unbefitting my age

My voice was strong and loud

My opinions true and proud

I wasn't really allowed

To truly be me

But I fought for myself

Read every book on the shelf

While I felt my mental health

Slip away

I'm played out with age

Time was wasted on me

I've invested too much

In I

I've been polite

Holding doors open

For everybody

Not just the good ones

I was always in trouble with the powers that be

But I kept on resisting, persistently insisting

That firecrackers are not gun shots

They requesting my favour

Seemed to think if my behaviour

Was left to fester

It may poorly reflect upon them

While I understand the inclination

When determining causation

Their poor interpretation

Was the only reflection

Now my voice, it has weakened

I've no real plans for the weekend

Even my week, it looks bleak

I wish I was young

And then I get to remembering

Just what it was like then

I wouldn't do that again

L.B.

Lenny Bruce was somewhere between a hero and a grifter.

He said "there's nothing more pathetic than an aging hipster."

I was young when I heard that around the time the movie "Twister"

Came out in the theaters, back then Paxton and Hoffman had vigor

Now they're dead and I am grey, young people call me "Mister"

They mean it real nice but to me it sounds sinister

Have you ever had a girl leave and you think how much you'd miss her

Thinking maybe you shouldn't have made a pass at her sister?

She gave you the warts, but she called them love blisters

If you could do it all again you'd have never even kissed her

And now it's too late to pray to Jesus, Allah, Lucifer

As you age you might become a better listener

You might run out of funds and become a shoplifter

A lot of aging folks feel above any suspicion

They just take what they need and if caught they blame
senility

They just fake for a moment that they have less ability

Than the young prick that's working in security

And he knows that busting an old lady would look so shitty

And he's got an eye on the clerk who he thinks is so pretty

He got into the job cuz he figured he'd be sitting

Around and getting paid while he went to university

He didn't sign on to be calling the cops on some old bitty

With some Werther's in her purse and a half pint of whiskey

But the boss was watching, and these jobs are in a scarcity

In this little town of twenty-one thousand three hundred fifty

So he took her to the back room, and he called the city

To come and pick her up, deferring the responsibility

They get paid better let them rob her of motility

The Poets

All the best poets are drunks

At least that's what the drunks will tell you

When they're drunk, anyway

The dingy rooms

Cheap tattered clothes

Tapping away at

Stained keyboards

Eliminating their filters

So they can write

Truth

It's all true

All the best poets are lawyers

Working all day

But the poetry comes out in the night

They struggle against their vocation

They prosecute

And defend

And mince thoughts

For their clients

Who can't speak their language

Which is intentionally

Obscure

All the best poets are birds

Singing songs from the branches

Intended only for their own kind

A language indiscernible

To anybody else

Yet they

Unconcerned

Sing on

All the best poets are unintelligible

Ragged and worn

Torn apart and broken

So, they can let you feel the pain

Through them

That you don't want to feel

But you do

All the best poets are our friends

They sent us a letter

And we sat and talked

We laughed

And the phrasings were pure those days

We should have written everything down

Jotted it all

Now it's gone

But the poetry lives now

Because it lived

Once

All the best poets fuck with the lights on

They have no air conditioning

Just a fan

And a wet towel

They read in the dark

They close their eyes when they drive

Just for a few seconds

Their hearts race

Danger

Thrill

All the best poets are

Whispering

Weird phrases

Odd word combinations

Into the ears of fallen gods

Asking impetuously

Thirstily

Laboriously

Is this good enough?

Do I need to be more?

Will the world know me one day?

All the best poets are lapdogs

Shameless self-promotion machines

Lubed with secretions

Charged through synapses

On fire from friction

Stuck in a prone position

Lying to their mothers

All the best poets are corporate managers

Wearing red ties

And hating themselves

They secretly blame their wives and husbands and partners
and children

For what they've lost

Not knowing

Or unable to know

That they gave it up

Themselves

They sacrificed the part of them

That made love

In the first place

All the best poets are pirates

And actors

Factory workers

Eating expensive grapes

Hurriedly

Guiltily

On their way home

They are tired of words

That fail them

And people who treat them the same

As they treat a waitress

And all the best poets are waitresses

Serving pancakes

With whipped cream

And thawed

Frozen

Strawberries

And powdered sugar

And butter

And syrup

And eggs

And potatoes

And they smell like the strong perfume

That they spray on

To kill the smell

Of the pancakes

And old frying oil

But all the best poets know everything

And nothing all at once

They speak to the masses

And to one

They hold me

Stroking my hair

And speaking in deep voices

About the tygers that roam the plains

It's hot

And it's raining

So it's steamy

And sweaty

And our ass crack is soaked

Like a security guard

In a bulletproof vest

At a Florida outlet mall

Off the 95

The droplets of us are

Tap, tap, tapping on the sidewalk

Like it's a drum

Or a loose plank of wood in an

Unstable stable

All the best poets aren't poets at all

They never put their beautiful

And horrible

Thoughts

Into words

Never write anything down

But lists

That they can check off

As their day spins away

From their life

My favourite food is the one on my plate

My favourite drink the one in my cup

And my favourite poet is the one I'm reading

Or the one I am with

My favourite poet is in this room

With me

Sometimes it is me

Sometimes it's you

And I suppose it can be

All of them too

All the best,

Ed

DISARTICULATED PRESS bubbled around in the brain of its founder, Greig Thomson, in the year after his time at the University of Adelaide. Meeting likeminded authors, equally disillusioned by the state of the publishing industry, Thomson decided to create his own literary press, to better serve the non-compliant, subversive, and widely ignored by the mainstream publishing brands. *Disarticulated Press* encourages voices with an edge, shouting to the skies or whispering into the darkness. All are welcome. To find out more, visit, *disarticulatedpress.com*